Robin and Rosie's New Room

Cockleshell Bay is a town near the sea,
With seagulls and sunshine and sand.
There are shops that sell ices and bright-coloured kites
That fly from a string in your hand.
There are white-painted houses along the sea front,
And one's called 'The Bucket and Spade'.
It's where people stay, and two children play,
With all the good friends that they've made.
So meet – Robin and Rosie of Cockleshell Bay.

Story by Brian Trueman
from the Cosgrove Hall series

Characters designed by Bridget Appleby
Backgrounds drawn by Avril Turner

For a while now, Mrs Cockle's tummy had been getting larger: another member of the Cockle family was on the way. So as to make space for the baby when it came, Robin and Rosie were going to move out of their room and up to the attic. Mr and Mrs Cockle had been getting it ready for them.

Finally, one spring morning, it was all finished. Mr and Mrs Cockle stood on the top landing. Robin and Rosie could come and see their new room. Mrs Cockle called to them: "Robin! Rosie! Hurry upstairs, the pair of you!"

"Your mother and I have something to show you!" explained Mr Cockle.
"Oooh! What?" said Robin and Rosie together.
"You'll see," promised Mrs Cockle.
"Put your hands over your eyes, and we'll steer you. And no peeping!" added Mrs Cockle.

So Mrs Cockle steered Robin into the middle of the room, and Mr Cockle followed with Rosie. "Now! Look!" she said.
"Wow! Gosh!" said Robin and Rosie, "Whee!" "Great!"
"Does that mean you like it?" Mr Cockle asked, smiling with amusement.
"Like it? It's great!" said Robin and Rosie together.

Suddenly Rosie spotted something. "Hey! Bunk beds!"
"Hmmm. We thought they'd give you more room for other things than your old beds," explained Mr Cockle.
"But how did you get them up here without us seeing?" asked Robin.

"I had them flown in by helicopter," said Mr Cockle, straight-faced, "and lowered down the chimney!"

"A helicopter! Wow!" said Robin. Rosie was more thoughtful. "But, Daddy! They wouldn't go down the chi . . . . . . Oh! Daddy! You're teasing!"

Mrs Cockle chuckled. "He certainly had you going there! We had them brought up while you were flying your kite down on the beach."

Then Robin had a sudden thought. "Hey! I bags the top bunk."
"Oh Robin! I wanted the top bunk!" replied Rosie.
"Well, I said it first."
Mr Cockle thought it was time to intervene:
"Two minutes in your new room, and you're having a row about it! Now, why don't you *both* have the top bunk?"

"There wouldn't be room!" objected Robin.
"Not both at once, chump! I mean, take it in turns!"
"Oh!" Rosie laughed. "All right, Robin, you can be first then!"
"No, you have it!"
"Oh crumbs!" said Mr Cockle. "Don't let's have a row about who's *not* having it!"
They all laughed.

Then Robin said, "Hey! What's that?"
He'd spotted a chest near the window.
"It's a toy-chest," explained Mr Cockle, "and it's got castors underneath so that you can move it around."

Robin sat on it, and tried. Rosie helped push him. "Hey! Ye-e-s-s!" they cried, driving it around like a go-cart. "Don't run us over!" laughed Mr and Mrs Cockle.

"Now, when it's in its proper place," continued Mr Cockle, "ahem, ahem – near the *window* . . ." – he paused while Robin and Rosie pushed it there – ". . . you can sit there and look out on the ships in Cockleshell Bay."
"Oh, yes!" agreed Robin and Rosie. "We can wave to the sailors."
"Yes," agreed Mrs Cockle. "What's more, we *got* it from a sailor!"

"Mr Ship!" Robin shouted. "It's from Mr Ship, isn't it, Mum!"
"Right first time!"
"Oh, great!" said Rosie and Robin.
"It certainly is," agreed Mr Cockle. "It means there'll never be any toys left lying about the house, ever again, doesn't it?"

"Yes," agreed both Robin and Rosie, earnestly.
"Says you!" laughed Mr Cockle. "But you like your new room?" he continued.
"Yes, it's great," said Robin and Rosie, both together.

"Can we go and see Mr Ship?" asked Rosie.
"And thank him for our toy chest?"
"Of course," said Mrs Cockle, and her husband added,
"I'll come and shout for you when lunch is ready."
So Robin and Rosie thundered off down the stairs.

As Robin and Rosie arrived in the yard, through the gap in the fence, they could hear Mr Ship singing to himself. "We sails to the East, We sails to the West . . . ." When they approached, he stopped: "Well, bless my barnacles! It's two of my crew, a-signing on for duty!"

"Hello, Mr Ship!" said Robin. "It's great!"
"Yes, it's lovely," Rosie agreed.
"Is it now? Well I'm glad to hear it!" said Mr Ship.
"But what are you talking about?"
"The *toy-chest*!" said Robin and Rosie together.
"Toy-chest?"

"Sea-chest – toy-chest!"
"Ah! Well you're very welcome, I'm sure!"
"Mmm! We can sit on it!" said Robin.
"And move it around," added Rosie.
"Yes. Well it's a pity it can't tell you stories as well!"

"Stories, Mr Ship?" asked Robin.
"Yes. Been on many a voyage that chest has. Been to the Baltic, with icicles hanging from the rigging, and down to the Indian Ocean, with monsoon rains, and across the China seas, where cut-throat pirates come up in their junks."

"Wow!" said Robin "I didn't know pirates sailed around on rubbish, Mr Ship!"
"Rubbish?"
"You said they sailed on junk."
"Not on junk. In junks. A junk is a kind of little fat boat with a big square sail, as they sail in those parts. And one night, I was giving my mate a hand with a roll of sail cloth – like a great big sausage – when pirates came aboard."
"Wow!"

"So we rushed at them with the cloth, and . . . whump! We knocked them flying. And then when they were down, we throws the cloth over them, and they're soon locked up below . . ."

"Crumbs! Gosh! Hurray!" gasped Robin. "Did you get a medal?"

"No, but the captain was so pleased, he gave me a sea-chest as soon as we got ashore."

"Gosh, Mr Ship! It's not . . . ."
"It is!"
"Wow! *Thank* you Mr Ship. But you can't . . . ."
"Why not? A present to me, now a present to you.
But see as you use it proper. I'll come and see your new quarters, and if they're not ship-shape, if the chest isn't full of toys, why . . . I'll clap you in irons!" he laughed.

So did Robin and Rosie. They thought they'd better go back and tidy up – and it would be time for lunch too.
"Goodbye, Mr Ship. And thank you!"
And they went back to the Bucket and Spade Guest House, and their new room, and their new chest.

Robin and Rosie are looking for their toys
to tidy away in the chest.
Can you help to find them?

This Thames Magnet edition first published in Great Britain 1986
by Methuen Children's Books Ltd
11 New Fetter Lane, London EC4P 4EE
in association with Thames Television International Ltd
149 Tottenham Court Road, London W1P 9LL

Designed by Susan Ryall
Printed in Great Britain
ISBN 0 423 01910 4
Cockleshell Bay is a Cosgrove Hall Production film series